DOMINO
THE CLUMSY CAT

Katie Seitz Weisenbarger
Art by Rachel Hathaway

For Leo and Mitchell
Inspired by Chris
-KW

For Jed
-RH

Printed in the United States of America

First Printing, 2018

ISBN 978-0-692-10953-3

IngramSpark Publishing

1246 Heil Quaker Blvd
La Vergne, TN 37086

www.IngramSpark.com

Visit Domino at www.DominoTheCat.com

Domino, the clumsy cat,
lives on a friendly farm.
His fur is black and white and
he is full of catlike charm.

Domino was strutting past
a lovely pasture pond.
He gazed at his reflection,
and he saw something was...

He bounded to the chicken coop
and yelled his feline holler.

"Help me, someone! Help me, please!
It seems I've lost my collar!"

The chickens clucked and flapped their wings.
One said, "Let's go! Let's help!"
Domino jumped up with joy
and gave a gleeful yelp!

The herd approached the giant barn
and trudged their way inside.

"ATTENTION, HORSES!
I NEED HELP!
MY COLLAR'S GONE!"
HE CRIED.

Neighs and clucks and meows ensued.
They rallied up to go!

"We must! We will!
We can! We shall!
We'll help you, Domino!"

To the field the group pushed on.
The sheep stood in a herd.

"Excuse me, please,"
said Domino.
    "A tragedy's occurred!

We're on a mission currently.
My collar's been misplaced.
It is a family heirloom
that can never be replaced!"

The leader of the sheep declared,
"We'll find what he has lost!
We will help our frenzied friend
no matter what the cost!"

The chickens and the sheep and the majestic horses, too,

all worked together tirelessly
to see the problem through.

They scattered and they scoured
every nook and every cranny.
The search that happened on that
friendly farm was just uncanny!

Not one chicken, horse, or sheep
could find a good result.

The rummaging and scavenging
had reached a sudden halt.

No one had found anything,
although their eyes were
PEELED.

They gathered back together
in that vast and friendly field.

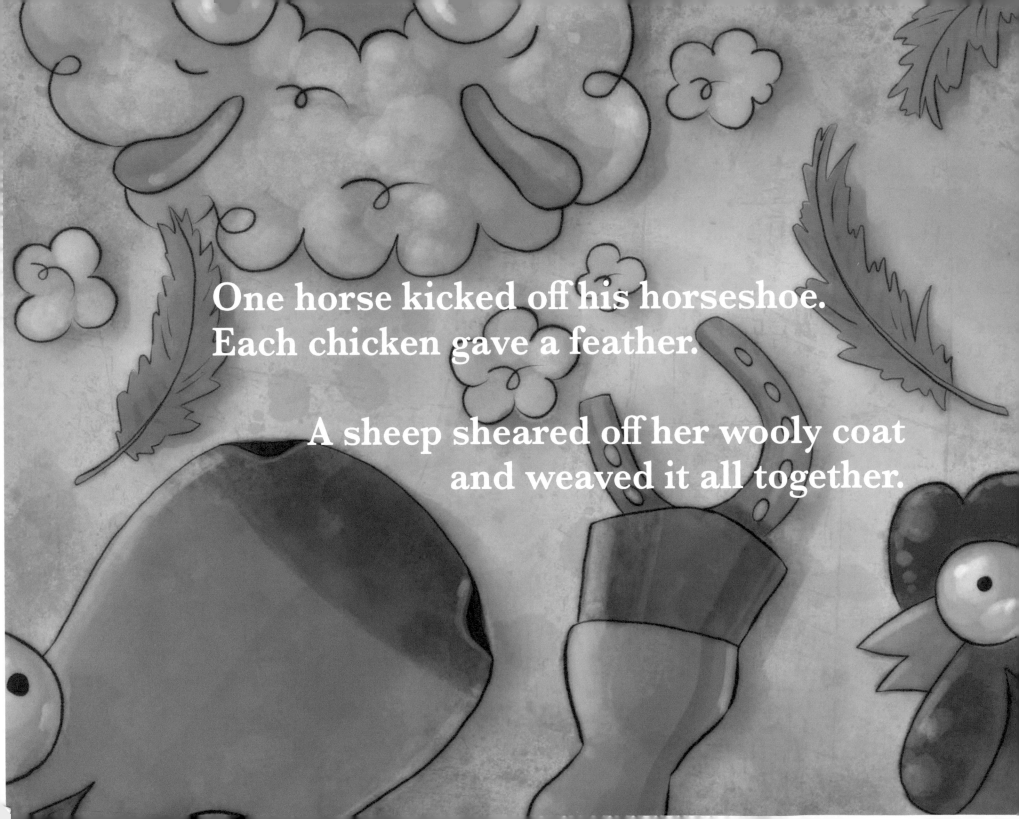

One horse kicked off his horseshoe.
Each chicken gave a feather.

A sheep sheared off her wooly coat
and weaved it all together.

They all assembled,
tied, and wrapped

a new, farm-friendly collar.
As they placed it on his neck,
Domino stood taller.

"Thank you, friends. It's beautiful."
They stared in wonder of it.
"This collar that you made for me, I absolutely love it!"

Domino strolled proudly home
as the herd began to part.

He gazed at his reflection
with his farm friends near his heart.